BIG**FAT**

Frat Party

Hedonist

Hedonist

CONTENTS

BIG FAT FRAT PARTY

Amber:

I'm not really into parties, but tonight I'm getting ready for one anyway. The reason? Frank.

Frank the Tank, as he's known around campus. His reputation precedes him, but perhaps not in the way he thinks. Otherwise, why would he keep going like this? Why continue to invite ridicule, unless… after the last addition to the not-so-secret YouTube channel the whole student body has been talking about, I'm convinced that maybe he doesn't know what's *really* going on.

People are fucking with him, and sooner or later someone - namely Frank - will get hurt. I won't be able to live with myself if I don't at least try to intervene.

The most recent video ended with Frank passing out face-down in the yard and the bystanders joking they were going to just leave him there all night, but not before emptying a large garbage can on top of him. Who knows how the next lot of videos will conclude?

Why bother getting involved, when Frank himself is making no efforts to save himself? He doesn't even know I exist. Still, I've developed a soft spot for him. And I would like to think that he's just a guy trying to have fun, and people are taking advantage of his easy-going nature. I'm convinced that's what it is. If I'm proved wrong and he's in on the joke, so be it. I'm still going to try.

By the time I get to the frat house, sporting the appropriately slutty attire, the party is well underway. It's the college lifestyle, supposedly. Binge drinking, and ill-advised hook-ups, all under the guise of getting a higher education. There's only one hook-up I have in mind for tonight, though, and my victim is already there.

I've never done this sort of thing, but God, do I want to.

Frank strikes an imposing figure. Six foot two, and quite rotund. He's got a big, round belly on him, which he likes to refer to as the keg, much to all the other guys' delight. Obviously. It might be a joke to them, but I think this part of his luxurious body is his best feature.

As far as party tricks go, Frank has established himself as being able to drink literally anyone else under the table. Chugging pitchers of beer? Call Frank. Funnelling? Frank's your man.

Being the slightly fucked up feeder I am, his capacity for putting away litres upon litres of fizzy alcoholic beverages has provided me with quite the spank bank. I've watched every single video numerous times, and tagged on a happy ending for myself in my imagination.

But even if he's the star of the YouTube channel named after him, someone else must be pulling the strings. Lately, the videos have shown a darker side which horrified me. The anonymous guy behind the camera has been egging Frank on to go *too* far. He's even announced upcoming pranks to be played on

Frank, which promise to do him even more harm than what his excessive (but mostly voluntary) drinking is already doing to him. That's what prompted me to come out tonight. Well, that and my naive hope that perhaps Frank will take a liking to me too, and who knows, I might get that happy ending I've craved for every time watching his channel.

Right now, the night is still young, though. Nothing has happened yet. People are mingling, everyone is putting away plenty of booze. Although I don't know anyone particularly well, no one seems suspicious. I've dressed the part. Scantily clad girls are always welcome at events like this. Nobody cares who I am or where I came from, as long as they can imagine they're getting some by the end of it all. Little do they know that I only have eyes for one guy; the one who's least expecting it.

I hang around for a while, have a couple of beers, and fight the insane urge to pounce on Frank right away. I liked what I saw in the videos, but nothing could prepare me for seeing the man in person. He's gorgeous. I don't know why I never tried to seek him out sooner. Sometimes it sucks being an introvert.

He approaches one of the sofas dotted around the room, and I quickly move in next to him.

"Hi!" I say. "You're Frank, right? Amber."

He glances at me and nods briefly. "Hi."

I literally have no idea what to say next. Well, that's awkward. Voila, the reason I never did this before has presented itself. I've got even less game than the furniture around here does.

Before I muster the courage to say anything else, a group of jocks arrive. Frank's eyes light up and they start to exchange some meaningless macho bullshit. Guess I didn't dress slutty enough for him, perhaps. Oh, the bitter sting of disappointment.

One of the newcomers offers me a drink, which I accept simply to have a reason to keep sticking around in the crowd. I do my best to answer his dull questions about what I'm majoring in, all the while making sure I look bored and disinterested enough as to not give him much hope.

Before long, something else grabs his attention and he lets me be.

It's time for the main event. This is what I wanted to witness tonight. Someone proposes a drinking game. Frank is eager to accept, and I'm partly excited and partly worried about what's going to happen next.

"He's good at this, huh?" I ask the guy who'd tried to flirt with me earlier. He shrugs.

"He thinks so, but perhaps he's not all that." His dismissive tone makes me suspicious. Could this be the mysterious cameraman from the channel? I'm not sure I recognise the voice, though.

A keg of beer is brought in, and distributed into dozens of cups. I feel my heart racing already. I'm about to see the show up close.

They set up a round of beer pong, or whatever it is. Frank doesn't need much prompting, so obviously he's picked as one of the players. This is what everyone is here for and he isn't about to disappoint his *buddies*.

The other guy is some football player I think I recognise, but can't put a name to. The game commences. I'm not sure what the objective is exactly, but both players are downing their drinks in quick succession amidst loud cheers and crude encouragements.

For a moment in between drinks, I feel Frank's eyes on me. My heart tries to jump out of my chest. Was he really looking at *me* just now? Maybe my outfit did get his attention after all. Or maybe he just noticed my thirsty stares, undressing him with my eyes.

Frank wins, of course. But more challengers line up, eager to join the game. I can't believe how much he's putting away in such a short time. And he hardly even looks buzzed yet. But from previous videos, I know that's about to change. He's got an ungodly thirst, but he's still human after all. He must feel rank in the morning after nights like this. And based on the regular uploads to his channel, I suspect that this has been going on almost every night lately. As impressed as I am by his capacity, I'm worried for him as well.

"Funnel challenge!" someone shouts.

More and more people start to crowd around, chanting his name.

Frank the Tank! Frank the Tank!

Again, I could swear he's glancing at me briefly, before making his way around the sofa and lowering himself down on it. It creaks dangerously underneath his weight. He smiles at his douchebag friends and nods. He's ready. Equal parts excitement and arousal overwhelm me. I wish I could feel what all that beer is doing to his already impressive gut. Isn't he getting full yet? It must be pretty firm to the touch by now.

I slip past some of the crowd and position myself right next to the sofa to watch up close. Sure enough, someone is mixing something into the beer they're about to pour into the funnel. I also overhear them saying something about 'taking his wallet and stuff' and that he's going to 'regret showing off'.

"What's that?" I whisper at some of the bystanders.

"Frank thinks he's so tough, he'll learn his lesson tonight. We're adding some vodka in his beer. There's no way he's going to keep up after that."

The other guy laughs and high-fives him.

As promised in the last video I saw, things are about to escalate.

I hold my breath and stare at him. Frank is talking to people, acting tough. But there's something off about the look in his eyes. Like he's not really there for it; not really enjoying himself anymore.

Although a part of me yearns to watch him drink it all, yet I also want to tell him he can stop if he wants. That they're cheating and that he has nothing to prove to anyone. But he couldn't possibly hear me over the loud chants from the crowd. And if one of the others realises I'm about to ruin their fun, they'll probably ask me to leave.

All I can do is watch as another football player guy faces off with Frank and they both down their funnelled drinks within seconds. Frank pats his big belly, and lets out a big burp. It's kind of hot how easily he did that. I'm conflicted; I was already wet for him, but I'm also getting concerned now.

Could he not taste the vodka? It must have gone down too quickly for him to realise.

Frank leans back against the sofa. His face is showing clear signs of intoxication as he tries to catch his breath.

Just at this moment, the cheerleading squad arrives in the other room, distracting quite a few of Frank's supposed buddies and luring them out of the room. I've got my chance.

I slip in past them and take a seat next to Frank on the sofa. It's cramped, next to him. And his weight has sagged the cushions so far down, I feel myself sliding closer to him almost without trying. It's difficult trying to maintain my composure now that I'm so close to the object of my desire.

"Hey, are you OK?" I ask, steadying myself with one hand on his shoulder.

His breathing is laboured. He must be starting to feel all that booze hitting him all at once.

"Great," he says. He lazily turns his head to look at me. His eyelids flag.

"You don't have to do this stuff if you don't want to."

God, I want him! Why do I want him so bad? It's making it hard to think straight.

He shakes his head. "It's just a bit of fun. Where did the guys go, anyway?"

The way he says it makes me sad. Like he thinks they're his friends, when actually they're not.

"I believe they're trying to score with the cheerleading squad at the moment. I'm not holding out much hope, though."

"You're not a cheerleader?"

I let out a little chuckle. "Me? Oh God, no."

"You're really hot. I assumed."

His eyes close again and he tries to breathe in deeply but it's obviously not working out so well. Still, his words embolden me to take things further. He thinks I'm hot at least! And here I thought he hadn't noticed me at all earlier.

I place my hand on top of his, prompting his eyes to open again, briefly. Now or never. It's time to put my nerves aside and make a move.

"You're not so bad yourself, Frank. Would you like to get out of here? With me?" I ask.

He pulls his eyebrows together. "What, like, alone?"

"Obviously, yes. Alone!"

He stares at my lips, then takes another deep breath. "Can't. I think I'm going to be sick."

I look around for some kind of receptacle for him to be sick into, but there's nothing to be found. Do I get up? I probably should save myself, but my legs aren't cooperating.

He's frozen in place with his eyes closed as well. Despite the music in the other room, all I can hear is the unnerving rhythm of his short, shallow breaths. He's really struggling now.

"False alarm," he says at last, while turning towards me. "This normally doesn't happen to me."

"They mixed vodka into your beer," I say, and bite my bottom lip.

His eyes widen. "No way. That's not fair!"

I shrug. "I'm sorry, I had planned to swap the drinks so the other guy would get it, but I never got the chance."

Frank lets his gaze linger on me for a moment. "You would do that for me?"

I'd do anything for you. Before I have the chance to come up with a sensible response, some of his idiot so-called friends return. Presumably their pick-up lines match their overall dickish demeanour and they were deservedly rejected.

Great, just when I was getting somewhere with Frank.

"This party is fucking boring," one of them complains.

"Those skanks don't know what they're missing."

I can't help but roll my eyes. The idiot who tried to hit on me earlier is the first to notice me sitting on the sofa.

"Hey Frank, why don't you introduce your new friend to the rest of us," he says, while pointing at me. One of the others already has his phone out. The mysterious cameraman reveals himself at last.

"Guys, this is Amber," Frank says. His words are starting to slur quite noticeably now. Still, at least he remembered my name. I'm taking it as a win.

By now, I'm pretty buzzed myself, and severely

distracted by his thick thigh pressed up against mine on the cramped sofa. I could ride the shit out of him right now, if only I had him all to myself. I don't even care that he's wasted. It would probably be so much hotter because of it. The prospect of his complete loss of control turns me on even more.

God, I'm a deviant, alright.

"Alright, how about we play a game?" the dude with the phone says. "Spin the bottle."

"That's ridiculous." I scoff. "What are you guys, twelve?"

He looks furious, more so when one of his greasy-haired buddies chimes in. "Yeah, why would we want to play spin the bottle with just one girl? I'm not making out with any of you homos!"

The homophobic slur he uses makes me roll my eyes even harder. These guys really are assholes.

"Okay, do any of you have a better idea, then?" he counters.

"How about a quiz. Loser has to drink a shot," another guy suggests.

I turn to Frank. The colour has returned to his face, somewhat.

"You don't have to stay, you know. My offer still stands," I whisper.

"Hey, hey, hey! No scheming, you two! We don't keep secrets from our brothers, ain't that right, Frank?" camera-bro says.

Frank glances at his 'friends', then gives me an apologetic look.

"Andy's right. We're brothers. Can't bail on them halfway through the party."

I shake my head in disappointment. As if any of them would give it a second thought, ducking out of a party early to get laid.

"Fine. If that's what you think. But I'm not joining your idiotic quiz."

It's with a heavy heart that I get up again, leaving Frank's sexy fat thigh, as well as the rest of him behind on the couch.

Shot down for the second time tonight. If he prefers their company over mine, it's his own funeral. I guess I'm still the same socially awkward nerd I was before all those drinks I downed. Despite my best efforts, he's just not that into me.

"Let's play truth or dare, except you have to alternate between the two, or it's boring as fuck," someone says. "You don't complete a dare or lie, and you have to take a shot of leftovers."

Like an idiot, Frank agrees. That's enough for me to leave the room. This is not going to end well.

I tried, didn't I? If he doesn't take the 'out' I've offered him, everything that happens now is his own fucking fault.

✳✳✳

I should have left the party altogether, but I didn't. Instead, I'm still hanging around the rest of the frat house, getting lost in the music, listening in on drunken conversations, helping myself to the occasional bowl of chips that nobody has spilled beer into yet. All the while, that same nagging feeling in my stomach follows me around like a persistent shadow.

Nothing has changed. Frank is still going to be in trouble. And he's unwilling to do a damn thing about it. I don't know why I can't leave it be, but something inside me refuses. I'm determined to hang around to play guardian angel, just in case. At the very least I want to catch another glimpse of him before the night is over.

Their stupid game of truth or dare must be well underway. What all they're daring each other to do, I can't even imagine. I probably don't want to know, anyway.

A loud cheer erupts from the other room. "Frank the Tank! Frank the Tank!"

Oh God, now what? I freeze and try to listen in to what else is being shouted, but the music is too loud. My heart starts beating faster, and I find myself slinking around the clusters of people dancing clumsily to the beat to get closer to the epicentre of excitement.

Frank staggers through the doorway, almost bumping into me. Fuck, he's tall. Though I'm still raw about him rejecting me, he takes my breath away and gets my juices pumping all over again.

"Sorry," he mumbles. Even though he's standing in place, he's still swaying dangerously side to side. Way drunker than he already was, if that's even possible. I'm pretty sure he's close to hitting his limits, if he hasn't already.

"It's okay," I say.

He stumbles in place and rests his hand on my shoulder to steady himself. "No, I mean, I'm sorry. It's a dare, so I've gotta ask."

I lean sideways and look behind him, only to find a smartphone camera pointed at my face, and the rest of the assholes watching with dumb grins on their faces. The douche brigade has arrived.

"What dare?"

"To make out with you," Frank says, then grimaces and shakes his head while looking down at the floor.

Although that's pretty much what I've wanted right from the start, I'm unimpressed. This is not how I wanted things to go.

"You guys dared him to make out with me?" I ask. "That's classy."

"Not technically," one of them says. He turns to his buddies. "I knew it! Frank's got a crush, you guys!"

The crowd whoops.

"Oh? So, what, *technically*, did you dare him to do, then?"

"To find the hottest girl at the party," Frank whispers. "Make out with the hottest girl at the party."

"That's funny." I glance up at him, then turn to look at our audience of idiots. Or it would be, if it wasn't also so fucking sad. If I'm so hot, supposedly, then why are we still here? Why aren't we alone somewhere, doing what I've been wanting to do all along?

"Come on, Frank! It's only a dare! You can always forfeit and drink this," the guy with the phone holds up a glass full of dubious looking brownish liquid with unidentifiable bits floating in it. "Leftover cocktail."

"Say the word, I'll drink it for you," Frank says. His eyes - though watery and unfocused - hold a certain tenderness I hadn't seen in them before.

Though I really shouldn't under the circumstances, I *do* still want to kiss him. Maybe even more so than before. It's the kindness in his eyes that convinces me.

"Don't be ridiculous. Who knows what those dickheads mixed into that glass," I grumble.

"I'm really sorry, Amber."

"If you'd listened and come with me earlier, we could have been doing this all along, without anyone else watching!" I complain.

His eyes widen and he sways in place again. He has no idea what I'm trying to tell him, does he? Short of flashing my tits at him, I don't know how I could be any clearer.

I reach up and wrap my arms around his neck. He leans down, almost losing his balance in the process. His breath smells like a brewery, but I'm pretty sure mine isn't much better at this point. What does it matter, I'm getting what I want, right? So fucking what if it's going to be recorded for all and sundry to see?

Our lips meet and my heart skips a few beats. His lips are soft, gentle, even a bit uncertain.

I cup his face and kiss him more firmly. It's everything I've craved for so long, and yet I can't fully surrender to the moment as long as we're being watched.

From the corner of my eye, I spot the guys who were

scheming to steal Frank's stuff earlier, and pull Frank closer to me by the waistband of his jeans. Then, I slip my hand into his pocket. Sure enough, there's his wallet, as well as a bunch of keys. I carefully remove both and sneak them into my handbag for safekeeping.

The guys cheer and laugh, no doubt thinking they managed to embarrass both of us with their clever challenge. Little do they realise I've been thinking about doing this all along.

Hopefully he's enjoying the moment as much as I am, even if he's wasted. God, will he remember it come morning?

He starts to get more into it now. His hands find their way onto my back then slip down and rest on my butt. His big, full belly presses into me, sending my mind and heart racing. Does he even realise how much he's turning me on right now? I want to do so much more than this. If only we were alone.

I pull back a little and look up at him.

"Are you done playing these silly games?" I whisper. "Can we leave now? There's a whole lot more we can do once we get out of here."

He whimpers and trembles slightly. His face turns red and slightly sweaty. His eyes dart downward, not sure at what exactly.

"Oh fuck," he stammers. "Damn, I'm so sorry!"

"What happened?" I ask.

Camera bro laughs, then points down at Frank's crotch.

"Oh, this is classic! Guys, Frank's done for the night!

What a loser."

I take a step back and find my eyes fixating on the dark spot on the front of Frank's jeans. He turns a few shades paler and stumbles backwards to get away from me.

"This is a stroke of genius, Brad! I can't believe this actually happened!"

I close my eyes and shake my head. They're going to have a field day with this video. Though, a part of me is impressed that he still managed to finish while being *this* wasted. I guess he really is into me after all.

"Fuck, Amber, I'm sorry," Frank mumbles.

He turns and hits his foot into a sideboard while trying to rush out of the room. He manages to regain his balance and leaves through the open doorway, no doubt rampaging through more furniture along the way.

"Very funny, guys," I remark. My sarcasm is met with roaring laughter.

"I can't believe it! Frank finally gets to kiss a girl and ends up blowing his load!"

"Marking his territory!" High fives and cheers all around.

I want to argue that that's not technically what happened, and none of it ended up on me, but there's no point. Fine, whatever. So, their grand plan to humiliate us both has come to fruition. It won't be long before this video goes live on the Frank the Tank YouTube channel and everyone on campus sees it.

I don't care. I don't have a *reputation* to take care of. All I can think about right now is that new titbit of information *Brad,* or whatever the fucker's name is, just let slip. Was this Frank's first kiss, ever? And he picked *me* to do it with. *Hottest girl at the party,* in his own words?

My heart is racing at the thought.

Then why has he been acting so fucking difficult? He was obviously interested, so why not just accept my invitation and take me home with him? We could have skipped past all of this nonsense and just had fun together. In private. As gorgeous as he might be, Frank's illogical behaviour continues to infuriate me.

And where the fuck did he run off to, now?

I force my way through the throng of douchebags and into the room I just saw Frank disappear into. No sign of him. I continue on until I find a locked bathroom door leading off the main hallway of the house.

"Frank, you in here?" I call out, knocking on the door. It's hard to hear over the music, so I press my ear against it and hold my breath.

"Go away! Leave me alone," he responds.

"Nope. Not going anywhere. Anyway, I need the mirror to fix my lipstick."

Inside, I hear the unmistakable sound of someone vomiting liquids. Frank the Tank has been defeated. I'm almost surprised there's no one here to record *this* memorable moment for the fucking channel.

That carries on for a little while longer, followed by the sound of the flush and a loud ruckus of stuff falling over.

"Hey, are you okay?" I ask.

"Piss off!" His previously deep pitch has shifted. He sounds like a cornered animal, lashing out at random. I can very well understand that he's upset. But I'm not leaving things like this. I'm not going to leave *him* like this.

"I won't. And you can't stay in there forever." I bang my fist on the door to make my point.

There's a little bit of a scuffle before the door unlocks. I try to push it open, but it won't go all the way. Although I'm pretty sure I won't like what's inside, I peep in anyway. Frank's sitting form is blocking part of the doorway. He's got his head in his hands and appears to be in tears or close to it.

As annoyed as I am with him, it still breaks my heart. Just why he insisted on letting things get this far, I'll never understand. All of this drama was wholly unnecessary.

The bathroom is a bit of a warzone. On his way down, he knocked the shelf by the sink off the wall, and all of its contents along with it. Although he's tried to aim for the toilet while throwing up, he's only been partially successful, so the floor is fucking disgusting as well.

Glad this isn't *my* house.

"Come on, can you get up?" I ask, while offering him a hand.

He blinks a few times while looking up at me, then swats my hand away. "Don't touch me!"

"Alright, I'm only trying to help!"

Jesus, he's a mess. His shirt is stained all the way

down his big fat belly, and obviously his jeans already had the wet patch from before. He reaches for something to his right, knocking the dustbin over as he does so. Not that it makes much of a difference to the state of the room.

When he raises his arm, I spot the bottle of whiskey in his hand, which he lifts to his lips to take a sip. Immediately, he starts to cough and splutter, causing most of it to dribble down his chin.

"Don't you think you've had enough yet?" I ask.

He glares at me. "I'm s-still awake, right?"

He's really starting to piss me off now. "Okay, you want to be a tragic hero, have it your way. But I'm not going to take a second more of this bullshit."

"Don't, then! Go away!" He raises the bottle again, undeterred by either logic or his own body's refusal to keep the booze down any longer. If he's trying to drink himself into a coma, he's doing a damn fine job at it.

But I'm not having any more of his shit. I snatch the booze from him before it even reaches his lips. He's so drunk, it isn't much of a challenge.

"Hey, the fuck!"

"Want it back?" I hold it in front of him and pull it away just as he tries to reach for it.

"Seriously. We're going home," I say. "Only then will I even consider returning this to you."

He tries to get up, but his shoes just slide around on the wet floor, leaving him stuck on his ass. Finally, he gets onto his hands and knees, and manages to heave himself up.

"Wash your hands." I point at the sink.

This time, he obeys my orders without further protest.

"Good. Now let's get the fuck outta here," I say, while shoving him out into the hallway.

Predictably, we're not alone anymore.

"Hey, love birds. Where do you think you're going?" Camera-bro sneers.

I give him a nice close-up of my middle finger.

"Aw, that's not nice! Frank, your skanky whore of a girlfriend is being a huge bitch."

Frank frowns. "Fuck you, Andy. Don't talk to her like that." Then he turns to me. "I'm sorry. Andy s- shouldn't say that."

I suppress a smile. Despite all his flaws - and there are many - deep down, he's okay.

"Alright, Romeo. Let's go," I mumble.

"Wanna turn out your bag for the camera, huh, Amber?" Andy says.

I glare at him. "The fuck did you say to me?"

"Well, seeing as you stole his wallet earlier. The camera doesn't lie." Andy holds his phone closer in my face. I try to swat it away, but he evades me.

"Whatever, bite me."

"You took my wallet?" Frank asks.

"You can have it back at home," I say. "Stop wasting time."

"Better count the contents, Franky boy! She'll take her payment for that kiss earlier, I can guaran-fuckin-tee it!" One of the others chimes in. The group laugh and cheer.

"Fuck these guys, seriously!" I grumble.

"Okay. Let's-s go," Frank agrees.

The douchebag crew is still talking shit behind us, but I tune them out. Trying to coax Frank out of the door without him bumping into stuff or falling over is difficult enough as it is. The confiscated bottle of whiskey falls to the floor somewhere along the way. Hopefully he'll forget about it before we get home.

Finally, we do make it outside and halfway down the lawn before bad luck strikes again. Or rather, Frank's insides strike, and I end up with vomit all over my shoes.

"Fuck!" That's what I get for trying to dress nice for tonight.

More laughter erupts from behind us. "Bull's eye, Frank! Aim higher next time, though."

"I'm s-sorry," he slurs.

"A little less apologising, and a little more walking, please," I plead. "Where do you live?"

He doesn't answer, but carries on staggering along the pavement, away from the party. After a few more steps like this, I decide to take the initiative again and get his wallet out of my purse. Luckily, his address is mentioned right there on his driver's license.

Armed with a renewed sense of purpose, I continue to walk him home. At first with one hand on his arm, guiding him forward, but when he starts to waver, I guide his arm around my shoulder, allowing him to balance against me a little. The added load makes it hard for me to keep walking straight, but we soldier on.

I try not to dwell on what he smells like for the rest of the way, but it's putting a damper on my spirits for sure. By the time we get to his place, I've got a plan in mind for what needs to happen next.

"My keys!" He pats down his pockets.

"Let me," I say, while fishing his bundle of keys out of my handbag. I knew these would be in better hands with me.

He watches me in silence. "S-stole my keys."

"Borrowed. For safekeeping," I correct him.

"You're s-sneaky."

"You're drunk."

"Okay." He leans against the doorframe and closes his eyes. I can see him sinking at the knees, so I shake his arm to get him to stay awake.

"In you go. Straight into the shower, you hear me?" I warn.

"Okay," he says, but he doesn't move until I put his arm back over my shoulders and usher him into the hallway. Thank fuck his place is on the ground floor. I don't know how I would have gotten him up a flight of stairs in his current condition.

"Where's the bathroom?"

He replies with a yawn, followed by a lengthy cough. He'd better not start throwing up again right here in the hallway! I'm ready to take care of him, but I draw the line at cleaning the carpet.

Finally, he starts to stumble forward. I wrap my arm around his thick waist and try to keep him steady. He's so heavy, he's almost immovable. Finally, we make it into his bedroom, and from there I shove him into the en-suite.

"Lemme sleep," he pleads. "S-so tired."

"Hell no. Strip off!"

He looks like he's on the verge of tears again. What suddenly set him off like this, I have no idea. Then again, he's wasted. Drunk people get this way sometimes, don't they?

"No!" he complains.

"I'm not going to bite," I say. "Just get into the shower."

He genuinely looks distraught, which surprises me. What's he so scared of? What does he think I'll do if he undresses in front of me? Take a video? That ship has already sailed.

"Tell you what. Show me yours, I'll show you mine," I suggest, while kicking my soiled shoes off into the corner by the sink.

That certainly has an effect. His eyes widen and he stares at me with his mouth agape. "S-riously?"

"Try me." I grin at him.

He starts fumbling with his shirt, prompting me to peel my top off. After the night we've had already, I certainly could use a shower as well. And if it helps me convince him to do the same, all the better.

"Fuuuuck me," he mumbles, when he steals a glance in my direction.

I'm tempted to grant his request, but that urge passes quickly. Not tonight. Not like this.

Before I know it, most of his stinky clothes end up on the floor. I pick them up and stuff them into an empty bucket in the corner.

"Go on. Underwear too!" I point at the bucket to make my point.

"And y-you?" he says.

Naughty boy.

I shrug, and wiggle out of my panties, and unclasp my bra. "Fine. Happy now?"

He can't stop himself from staring. I've got him exactly where I've wanted him before tonight even began; mesmerised. Except, I'm severely distracted by his naked form as well. Soft and fluffy all over, the best comparison for him would be if the Michelin man was a real person. Four hundred pounds of sexy - give or take- with a dick to match. Because as gloriously thick as the rest of his body is, his manhood doesn't disappoint either. Under better circumstances, I know he could pleasure me in every way I need. He's everything I thought he would be and more.

I turn on the water and wait for it to reach an acceptable temperature, then I usher him into the cubicle.

"Into the shower you go. Shoo!" I say, while glancing at his crotch. Are my eyes deceiving me or is it getting bigger?

Just when I try to step away to give him space, he grabs my wrist to stop me.

"Why?"

I'm captivated by his light brown eyes, which mostly

focus on my face, despite darting downward once or twice at my naked chest as though he can't help himself. I can very well understand. I'm severely distracted by the sight of him too.

He's the sort of guy who looks like he's always been fat. His gut isn't hard, or solid like what older guys tend to look like when they suddenly put on weight. It's all jiggly and pliable and perfect, like this is how he was meant to be. My fat prince.

"Why- what?" I mumble.

"Why are you here?"

I shake my head. There's no point in having this conversation. "Soap up. Unless you want to sleep on the bathroom floor?"

He bites his lower lip, reminding me of just how hot our first kiss was, before everything went horribly wrong. And oh my God, things went wrong on so many levels.

I make a quick escape and grab his toothbrush and paste from the shelf by the sink. "Here, you'd better brush as well," I tell him.

"Okay."

If all the booze has made his true self come out, then I'm in luck. He's the sweetest, most docile drunk I've ever come across, which is incredibly lucky considering how much of a risk I'm taking just by being here. Alone with a man three times my size, whom I don't even know. Naked. Dripping wet. Completely vulnerable. And yet, I feel safe.

In fact, I feel like I'm the one taking advantage of

him right now. I've wanted him naked all night, and I've got my wish now, though not for the reasons I'd fantasised about. It's damn hard keeping my hands to myself.

Predictably, the shower takes a little while and doesn't pass without incident. I end up joining him in the cubicle after he drops his soap, his toothbrush, his shampoo… It's obvious he can't do this on his own tonight. And anyway, he's so big, it's probably hard for him to reach every bit of his body that needs attention even when he's sober. So, I happily volunteer to help out. Out of the goodness of my heart; partially, anyway.

Once he's all wet and slippery, I soap him up properly. Every little fold and roll gets washed carefully before rinsing the foam back off. I already knew he was gorgeous and would be hard to resist simply from the videos, but now… *Jeez*.

My pussy is clenching with arousal and I can't even do a damn thing about it. Well, I *could*, but I don't want to just yet. I try to enjoy our moment in the shower together without getting ahead of myself.

Somehow, I've managed to get us both cleaned up, and he's still standing - barely- by the end of it. He drops his towel on the floor as well for good measure, prompting me to step in yet again. I rush a little to dry him off. This continued closeness is having an effect on both of us and I'm dangerously close to losing control.

Initially I'd rejected my observations as mere suspicion on my end, but by now he's got a full-on erection going too. It excites me beyond belief, even if

I'm trying my best to ignore it.

Nothing would be easier than to take him right now. To use his luxurious body to fulfil my dirtiest fantasies. There's no way he'd refuse; perhaps he'd even fall asleep halfway through, leaving me to defile his unconscious body for as long as I desire. I'm slick just thinking about it, but I don't act. When I take him for the first time, I want him to be all there for it. I want his permission as well as his participation. It'll be a night to remember. For either of us.

"I'm sorry," he mumbles.

"For?"

He gestures down at his crotch. "It's dispect- disrespectful."

"Don't worry about it." In any case, I'm taking it as a compliment.

"You're nice. Why are you being nice?"

Ulterior motives? I smile up at him and tug at his arm. "Let's go to bed."

"Okay."

Every time he says it like that, my heart jumps a little. I never realised how much of a sucker I am for all this submissiveness. Frank is making me realise all kinds of new stuff about myself. Guess I'm an even bigger pervert than I thought.

I watch him shuffle out of the en-suite and towards the bed. It's a small double, with an even smaller comforter. His place definitely isn't set up for sleepovers. The thought that I might be the first girl he's ever had in here makes me stupidly happy.

It takes him a few tries to put on the t-shirt that's already lying on the bed. Meanwhile, I borrow another from his wardrobe for the same purpose, then continue staring at his fat ass while he finally pulls up his shorts. Damn, he's hot. Too bad I can't do anything about it just yet.

The bed creaks rather loudly underneath him when he sits on the edge, but it holds even as he loses his balance and falls backwards onto the mattress. Loud, laboured snores erupt the moment his head touches the pillow. He splutters and coughs a few times, then carries on snoring. I'm left to deal with the comforter that's trapped underneath him, and his tree-trunk-like legs which are still hanging off the edge.

It takes a few tries, but finally I've got him positioned on his side, facing the edge, just in case he gets sick again. His breathing grows easier, deeper, and I can relax. I take a moment to caress his hair and just look at him. Despite everything that's gone wrong tonight, I still think he's gorgeous. Our first kiss was anything but perfect, but it's making me yearn for more. *Way* *more.* Maybe, hopefully, by morning I'll get the chance to satisfy every one of these urges.

I position myself behind him, with one arm across his ample stomach, just to make use of what little space there is under the small blanket. Although my pussy is still aching for release, it doesn't take long for me to settle in too. While listening to the regular ins and outs of his breaths, I slip away within minutes.

Frank:

I wake up rough, just like every other morning. The intense headache, the feeling that something died deep inside my stomach, and the heaviness in my chest and extremities; it's all exactly as usual. Still, something's different today as well.

It takes me a minute to find my bearings. Not bad. I've woken up in my own bed this time, and despite the debilitating hangover, I feel… somewhat *fresher* than normal, maybe?

The scent of shampoo clings to my pillow, though there's something else mixed in which I can't identify. My mouth is dry as expected, but when I run my tongue across my teeth, I find that they're smooth; clean, which is unusual.

Only when I feel an alien twitch on my side, do I realise the full extent to which this morning differs from every other one I remember lately.

I'm not alone.

Although it's not a sensation I've ever felt before, the warmth along my back should have tipped me off. Gentle breaths, tickling my shoulder blades, and an arm, draped across my side, as if it's the most natural thing in the world.

What the fuck happened last night?

I try to remember, but the drone of my racing heart

won't let me focus. I carefully reach for the arm, trying to determine the identity of the person still asleep behind me. Who is this, in my bed?

A slender wrist awaits. It's most definitely a *she*. Rings grace two of her elegant fingers.

She stirs, causing me to freeze in place only part of the way through my exploration of the mystery arm. Those fingers I'd just caressed part, and thread through mine.

Despite the foul head- and body ache, despite this excruciating hangover, the moment electrifies me. It heightens every one of my senses. I don't even know what the girl looks like, but I'm rocking shorts-full of morning wood for her regardless. I yearn to reach down and get rid of it before she wakes up properly, but it feels like a violation. I couldn't possibly do that with her right behind me. It'll have to wait until I make it to the bathroom.

Did we *do it* last night?

That question cuts like a two-edged sword. On the one hand, I've been dying to finally get laid, so that would be a cause for celebration. On the other, I mourn the loss of those precious memories, just in case it never happens again. Because whatever happened in the fog of alcohol last night, is bound to horrify her now that she's sober.

God, I hope I didn't take advantage of her.

She coos softly, and stretches her legs against the back of mine, sending shivers down my spine. The arm which both terrified and comforted me earlier, is pulled away, leaving nothing but emptiness in its wake. The moment is lost and reality is about to rear its ugly head.

I hold my breath and try to turn around, but there isn't a whole lot of space, so I stop part of the way before I risk crushing her.

She yawns; that's what it sounds like, anyway.

"Morning, Frank," my female companion speaks in a voice I'm not sure I've heard before. Well, at least she doesn't sound too upset. And she knows my name, even if I don't remember hers yet.

My eyes are growing more used to the dimmed light and I can't contain my curiosity any longer. I turn the rest of the way and fight through the resulting dizzy spell brought on by my hangover.

She's gorgeous. In a familiar sort of way. But I can't remember just yet where I've seen her before. A heart-shaped face framed by wavy ash blonde hair. Her light-coloured eyes sparkle as she smiles at me.

I must be dreaming. This sort of thing just doesn't happen to guys like me.

"I'm sorry," I start.

"You apologise a lot. Has anyone ever told you that?"

Do I? What have I been apologising for? My heart is still racing and my memory is failing me.

"I think I drank too much last night."

"No shit, Sherlock." She grins again. It does something funny to my heart.

This beautiful woman went to bed with me last night. *Me!* And I can't even remember a second of it.

What a complete waste.

"You'll have to remind me of what all I've forgotten."

She makes a face. "Be careful what you wish for."

Does she have to speak in riddles? I shake my head, and immediately regret the movement. "Oh fuck, my head," I grumble.

"Hang on." She starts to get up.

I want to stop her, just to stretch this magical moment out a little bit longer, but the incessant pounding behind my eyeballs won't let me. All I can do is press my fist against my forehead and wait for it to stop. Meanwhile, I'm alone again.

Perhaps I did just imagine it all, because there's no way any girl would react positively to waking up next to the likes of me; never mind one as beautiful as her. There has to be some mistake.

A minute or two pass and footsteps stop by my bedside.

I open my eyes to find her standing there holding a humongous beer mug - a souvenir from last year's Oktoberfest, and a little pink pill in her outstretched palm.

"Take this. You'll feel better."

I try not to focus on the silhouette of her boobs under the flowy cotton t-shirt and instead stare at the pill. What is she giving me? Do I even want to know?

"Relax, it's only a painkiller!" she says. How does she know what I'm thinking? Am I accidentally voicing out all my thoughts?

She doesn't respond to that, leading me to conclude that my inner monologue is still intact after all.

"Thanks," I mumble, while carefully swinging my legs off the bed to sit up. Oh fuck, the room starts spinning again. Placing my bare feet onto solid ground helps somewhat.

I take the pill and wash it down with a few sips of water. It tastes a bit funny. Sweetish, salty-ish, but not at all unpleasant.

"Finish it, Frank, the Tank!" she says. "You'll need those electrolytes."

I shoot her a surprised look. She knows my nickname too? Fuck, of course she does. Just because *I* don't remember what happened last night doesn't mean she's brain damaged too.

Her eyes widen when I raise the mug to my lips again and down the full three pints in a few giant gulps.

A fragmented memory enters my mind. She was there at the party and watched me during the funnel challenge.

She had that same unusual expression on her face even then. That look of anticipation in her eyes, as though she's holding her breath, waiting for me to finish. *Almost as if she likes to watch me?* I reject the thought as soon as it enters my mind. I'm a freak show and I know it.

"You were there last night," I say. "At the party."

"That's where we met," she says.

Sure enough, that loosens up another little memory of her. How could I forget her? She was the most beautiful girl there. Probably even the most beautiful girl I've ever seen. We chatted a few times throughout the night. Some of the stuff I remember her saying doesn't quite seem right. About getting out of there together. Maybe that part was just a dream. Then again, she's here at my place now, isn't she, so maybe we did exactly that?

"Amber."

She smiles. A perfect row of white teeth appears. "You remember!"

"Don't get too excited, that's pretty much all I can recall," I complain. I really wish I could distinguish between actual memories and wishful thinking.

"I have a way to jog your memory, but you're probably not going to like everything you see." She chews her lip, distracting me some more.

I wonder what those lips taste like. My subconscious tries to convince me she tastes of vanilla ice cream. Not sure how I came to that conclusion, because she couldn't have possibly let me anywhere near that perfect mouth of hers.

She sits down next to me, with her thigh pressed up against mine. The resulting heat I feel even through the sheets threatens to drive me wild, but she seems completely unaware of what she does to me. I'm such a creep. Pathetic.

I fold my arms to hide what's going on underneath the blanket. The last time I woke up this hard, I must have been about fifteen years old. And I can't do a damn thing to alleviate this ache with her still in the room. It's a sweet sort of torture, if only it wasn't also so fucking shameful.

"I suppose I'll find out eventually, anyway," I mumble. "Good and bad."

She shrugs and hands me her phone. "Although I haven't checked yet, I assume they would have uploaded some stuff by now."

I put the mug down on the bedside table and scroll through the entries of the YouTube feed she's showing me. The channel's name? *Frank the Tank.*

My heart sinks. "Oh fuck."

Her hand ends up on my thigh, making me flinch. Even the sting of humiliation isn't enough to rid me of my hard-on completely.

"I'm sorry you had to find out like this," she says.

There are a ton of videos. All of me, from the looks of it. Some are regular party scenes; chugging beers, arm wrestling, and drinking games. But some are much, much worse. The captions are brutal, especially the ones on the most recent uploads.

I pause on one of the last. *'Truth or dare with Frank the Tank Pt 3: Pathetic drunk fatso jizzes his pants while making out with sorority skank!'*

"Oh fuck," I whisper.

"I tried to tell you last night. Those guys aren't your friends."

"Andy did this?" I ask, pointing at the phone? "No way!"

"I don't remember those losers' names. Turn up the volume, you'll probably recognise the voice."

I shake my head. "No fucking way."

She gets up again and picks up the giant mug, before leaving me to it. Although whatever little hope I'd woken up with has vanished without a trace, I can't help but stare at her shapely figure, walking away from me. Is she naked underneath that old t-shirt of mine?

Once she disappears through the hallway, all I've got left for company is the phone with those infernal clips. I play one after the other. It hurts deeply at first: the betrayal. But soon enough, I just feel numb.

I could use a fucking drink though, that's for sure.

When I'm finally done browsing the dozens of recent entries, I look up and find her waiting in the doorway with a fresh refill of water in her hand.

"Are you okay?" she asks.

Her voice sounds flatter now; thinner. A vulnerability which she hadn't shown before. I'm not sure I can trust it. After everything I've seen, I'm not sure *who* I can trust anymore.

"You took my wallet and keys," I say, remembering an outtake from the worst video of the lot.

"Only because I overheard one of your so-called friends say *he* was going to, just to fuck with you. I put them in the bedside drawer for you."

I'm lost for words. I kissed her. I can't believe I actually kissed her and she kissed me back. It would have been so perfect, if not for the humiliation that followed... *Fucking hell.*

"Why?" I ask, finally.

"Because I'm not a thief, that's why!" She folds her arms.

I shake my head. "No, not that. Why are you still here? After everything I did to you last night."

"You didn't do anything to me; not really," she says.

Tears sting against the corners of my eyes. I point at the phone and hold it up to show her. "It's all right here. I sought you out on a dare. I assaulted you in front of everyone. I humiliated you on camera. You're going viral on YouTube because of *my* stupidity!"

"*That's* what you're most worried about? That I'm in a dumbass video with you?" she asks.

"Everyone's going to be talking about this. Don't you get it?" Numbness has made way for anger. I'm outraged on her behalf. Is she *trying* to commit social suicide? Why didn't she refuse? Why didn't she knee me in the crotch when I dry-humped her during that kiss?

She shrugs and takes a few steps in my direction. Doesn't she care? Does she have no sense of self-preservation at all?

"What are you still doing here? Please just leave me alone right now. Take your phone and go home," I say, handing her the device.

She stops barely two feet away, but then she carries on and puts her hand on my shoulder. Her touch stings against my skin. It threatens to crush my heart to a pulp, so I try to shake her off.

"Just go, okay?" I plead.

"That's what you said last night too. But just as you shouldn't have been alone last night, I don't think you should be right now either."

Does she have to be this fucking stubborn? Why are

we even still dragging this shit out? If she's here out of pity, we might as well put a stop to it right now.

"What's the difference? I've always been alone, and even when I thought I wasn't, it turns out I still was. The butt of every joke as usual. Don't you worry about me, I'm quite used to it."

"Look, I know what betrayal feels like," she whispers. "And I realise that I don't really know you, and you don't know me, but when people hurt me in the past, I know I could have used a friend."

I scoff. "A friend. Sure! There's no such thing as friends."

"I know it feels that way. Just…" She sighs.

"What?" I snap.

"Can I at least give you a hug?"

"What's that going to solve?" I complain. "Spare me your pity!"

"There's a difference between empathy and pity, you know! And there's no need to be shitty about this." Her sharp tone makes me flinch.

Although I want nothing more than to be alone in my misery, when I look up, I start to change my mind. Seeing her standing there with her arms tentatively stretched out, and a lone tear rolling down her cheek, I can't shoot her down any longer. I simply choke. Despite everything, she's still trying to be nice to me. *Why?*

Then again, what have I got to lose?

And when she places her hands on both my shoulders, and nudges me towards her, I break down and accept her kind gesture. I let her wrap her arms around me and surrender to her sweet embrace. With both eyes shut, I inhale her intoxicating scent, and bury my face in her chest while her arms surround my head and neck. For some strange reason, she doesn't fight it.

She positions herself between my legs and lowers herself down onto my lap. It takes my breath away. I lose myself when she runs her hands through my hair and nuzzles her face in it.

It's a beautiful moment, comforting, heart wrenching, and oh so very sexy, even though perhaps it wasn't meant that way. Her shapely ass on my thigh. Both our bodies pressed up against one another, closer than any other person has ever come to me.

The contrast between us is striking. Like beauty and the beast; and it's obvious which one I am, and yet she doesn't show even a hint of disgust.

"It's going to be okay, Frank," she whispers. "Everything's going to be fine."

Before I know it, I've got my own arms wrapped tightly around her petite body. My belly crushes up against her svelte frame. Her round breasts, temptingly bra-less underneath the borrowed t-shirt, press into me, and send my heartbeat soaring to a feverish pace. My hands twist and weave through the soft locks of her blonde hair. My lips, slightly parted, are unable to resist the temptation of the silky skin on the side of her neck any longer.

I kiss her, cry into her, drink in her scent and dig my fingers into her back in an attempt to absorb her fully in my embrace. Gone is the numbness, gone is the surreal sense that all of this has been happening to someone other than me. There are only two people here, and one of them is so beautiful, the likes of me shouldn't even be permitted to look at her, never mind touch her as I am right now.

It's a forbidden dream; one someone like me doesn't deserve to have. And yet she doesn't fight it. She doesn't freeze up or retreat as part of me continues to expect. Instead, she tightens her arms around me as well and capitulates.

Gone is any semblance of self-control on my part. My cock springs back from its earlier semi-flaccid state and comes to life even harder and prouder than when I first woke up next to her. Can she feel it, pressing into her thigh? She must, and yet she doesn't flee from its presence.

God, how much I want her right now. Never have I felt this way before. Never have I had even a taste of this kind of yearning. So strong, it could break me. My life, my happiness, lies in her hands now it seems. I'll live and die at her word.

I remember flashes of last night. So much happened; things that weren't captured on film. The memories haunt me like a feverish dream. When she had me strip off before stepping into the shower. I couldn't even hide it from her anymore and it almost brought me to tears then too. This recollection deepens my newfound shame. She washed me, towelled me off, and put me to bed. Who does that for someone they've only just met?

Why would someone do that for *me*? After seeing me at my worst. After humiliating her in front of everyone at the party. I'm so unworthy, it hurts again.

"I'm so sorry," I cry.

"You've got to stop apologising to me," she whispers, before nibbling on my earlobe and planting sweet kisses on the side of my face. It tickles me inside and out. I hope she won't ever stop.

"You took care of me last night. Why would you do that?"

"Because I wish that if I needed it, someone would take care of me too."

I shake my head and pull back to get a better look at her face. "No, in that case you could have just dropped me home and left. You did so much more."

She smirks through her tear-stained lashes. "Okay, so I might have had an ulterior motive."

I study her eyes. Those vulnerable, blue-green eyes which continue to stare into mine.

Even last night at the party I noticed the way she looked at me. It unnerved me, because I didn't know what I was seeing, except that it was different. There was a kindness in her gaze. Appreciation. Perhaps even admiration. These are things I'm not used to seeing in other people. Ever. Everything she shows me is new.

"What motive is that?" I speak in a whisper so low; I can hardly hear myself.

"Because… I really like you."

Those four little worlds blow all my fuses. I'm blinded, deafened, incapacitated all at once.

She cups my face, just like I vaguely remember her doing before that very first, very drunken kiss. I can't breathe, nor think. All blood flow has been diverted from my brain, to… elsewhere.

Fresh tears stream down my cheeks. It's embarrassing, yet she doesn't seem to care. She leans down and presses her mouth up against mine. Sweet, soft, sensual lips. The faint aroma of vanilla ice cream overwhelms me.

My memory, though patchy and unreliable, was not mistaken about this. Even though I was beyond wasted, our first kiss had etched itself in my mind forever. It just took a little reminder to coax that memory free.

Her tongue seeks me out, hungry as it is for mine. Her hands travel downward, from my cheeks down my neck and shoulders, onto my chest. I want to tell her not to. That she doesn't need to touch all these ugly parts of me, but I dare not break away. Just her kiss is enough to capture me.

This moment is pure magic. Her touch, confident and persistent, has arrived at my man boobs. So big and grotesque, there's even a video on that godawful YouTube channel where I'm passed out and the guys are trying to fit me for a bra. I don't recall the exact size, except it was a DD.

And yet she doesn't hesitate; her little hands knead them gently at first, then seemingly weigh them against her palms, just like what a guy might do to a girl. She moans and kisses me firmer, before carrying on exploring the rest of me by touch. From my chest down to *the keg*. She carries on loving my flabby, overgrown body with her hands in ways I never dreamed possible. All the while, our lips never part for more than a breathless second; in fact, her movements are speeding up and getting more intense the further she goes.

"Frank, you're so sexy," she moans.

I'm about ready to explode. How is she doing this to me? How does she know exactly how I need to be touched better than I do myself? Because I sure as hell would have never insisted on any of it. I would have preferred she keep her hands away; avoid this awkwardness. And I would have been so wrong.

She must obviously be lying about how she feels, and yet… Everything she does proves the opposite. That she's really into me, physically. She rubs, caresses, fondles and squeezes me; every little part of my giant body, which so far had never known a woman's touch. It makes me shiver and squirm and rejoice all at once.

I've worn this body like armour for most of my life. Like a regular guy in a fat suit, I attempted to hide the real me and keep the world out. Whatever touched the outside-the insults and even assaults I've faced over the years- none of it was ever meant to reach the core of who I really am. If only I grew big enough, I thought I'd be safe.

I knew what I needed to do to lose it; I'm not stupid or naive. But I never did follow through, because that would have missed the point. Instead, I kept on pushing the boundaries of my appetite. I made it into a sport. Food became my first love; I ate as often and as much as I could possibly cram into myself. Until the pounds added up by the dozens, and I grew into someone I barely recognise anymore.

And then when starting college, drinking took over, at least at night. I was racing to grow my armour thick enough so that nothing could ever penetrate it. It didn't directly give me joy, but it stopped me from *feeling* all that much. But now she's breaking down all these barriers and defences. She's making me aware of things I didn't know I could perceive.

And how is my cock getting ever closer to its inevitable release without even a hint of direct manipulation? This is exactly what happened last night, when I ruined our first kiss.

I carry on kissing her and she continues to let me. She makes the cutest little noises; moaning into my mouth with every ragged breath. Almost squealing when her hands find a particularly squishy part of me on her journey of tactile exploration.

I buck my hips into her and it sends an electric jolt right through my heart. Oh, I can't fucking take it any longer, or my chest might explode.

"Amber, I want you so badly," I groan. Now, where the fuck did all this courage come from?

She pulls back for just a moment and smiles at me. Her pretty face could make me cry it's so pure, and yet I've begun to imagine unspeakable things I want to do to her. *With her.*

"Finally. We're on the same page," she says. "I've had a really hard time holding back."

Before I get the chance to say or do anything else, she pushes me backwards until I lose my balance and land on my back on the bed. I'm helpless now, weighed down by my own limitations, and completely at her mercy.

She lifts herself off me just for a moment, then releases my aching cock from the tight grasp of my shorts. Sweet relief washes over me. It's happening so quickly; I can't even be sure it's real or imagined. My first time, with the most gorgeous girl I've ever had the privilege to lay eyes on? Or is it the second time now? I really can't be sure anymore and neither do I wish to question it.

I'm so close, I'm about ready to burst. Salvation is within reach; I can almost taste it.

She doesn't waste any more time before mounting me.

There is no foreplay as such, no hesitation on her part. She just grabs my cock and unceremoniously lowers herself onto it. Evidently, she *was* naked underneath that shirt. The sensation is indescribable. Naked, hot, wet and slippery. Amber lets me enter her fully. Her slick pussy accommodates me with ease, and yet… It grips my shaft tightly, sending my thoughts spiralling into chaos.

Utter perfection.

I almost cum right there and then, but with a few deep breaths and some focus, I manage to get myself under control. There's no way I'm going to let this precious moment pass too quickly this time. It almost hurts to stop the inevitable, but I grit my teeth and do it anyway.

"Oh Frank, you're even better than I imagined," she groans, while starting to rock her hips back and forth on top of me.

I can't believe how good this feels. Despite the uncontrollably jiggle in my fat body, highlighting just how inadequate I am compared to her. And yet… It's unbelievable how fucking horny *she* appears to be throughout all of this. As though it was all *her* idea and not mine.

"Will you fill me up, Frank?" she asks. "You're going to shoot a huge load into me, aren't you?"

She's making it sound like I'm doing her a favour instead of the other way around. Still, I can't help but play along. A sense of pride fills me; she's awoken my dormant ego along with my cock.

"Oh, fuck," I grunt. "Hell yeah, I will!"

She starts to ride me a little faster. Her little hands try to peel my t-shirt off my huge, wobbly belly. *The keg* is a running joke among everyone who knows me; its nickname is one I came up with myself as a tiny attempt to control the narrative. Fat load of good that did me. It wasn't meant for any of this. My body doesn't deserve to be on display, especially not now, in front of her, and yet she can't stop touching me like she owns me.

"Oh, I love it, Frank. I love your big, sexy body," she moans.

My eyes snap shut and I try to breathe, but fail. She can't possibly be serious, and yet I'm convinced that she means every word.

"You're mine now. Tell me you're all mine. Tell me I'll never have to share all this with anyone else!" she insists.

My mind goes blank. Although I want to answer her - to tell her I'll be her slave forever if that's what it takes- I can't do much more than groan and pant desperately to try and keep up with her insane rhythm. She could ask me for the world and I would be unable to refuse.

My cock is starting to squirm and pulsate. I can feel the onslaught of my orgasm. It's so close now, there's no hope of stopping it or delaying it much further.

"Yes!" I cry out. "I'm yours, Amber!"

She's still bouncing up and down on top of me. Faster, harder, tits swinging freely underneath the soft cotton t-shirt. The vision drives me crazy. More so, because I can't muster the energy or courage to reach out and touch them. How I want to taste them; love them as I do the rest of her.

She slams down into me once or twice more, and cries out my name on the top of her lungs.

"Oh fuck, Frank!"

Something changes. She's no longer moving, but her pussy continues to. It grips me tightly until I can't stand it anymore. My body reacts violently, shooting a big load deep into her willing body. She flops down on top of me, as I shudder and pant uncontrollably. Shivers travel across my sweat-stained skin. Her arms tighten around my neck and her lips seek me out again.

I want to kiss her. I try to, but it turns into a sloppy mess. She's equally lost, so it doesn't seem to matter. Hot breaths brush against my face as she takes my bottom lip into her mouth and sucks on it.

Her hips tremble against me. Her pussy contracts a few more times, as if her body is hungry to receive every last drop of my seed. I'm much too happy to oblige. She didn't even make me wear a condom. Why not?

I wrap my arms around her spent little body, and caress her back until she catches her breath and I catch mine.

"That was amazing," she whispers.

I don't know what to say, but realise that I've already got a big smile on my face. The pain I'd felt just moments ago, it's all but forgotten. I've woken up from a nightmare, fresh like never before. Even my headache has faded.

This was undoubtedly one of the worst mornings I can remember, and then on a dime, everything changed. Thanks to Amber, and her refusal to listen to my idiotic attempts at shooing her away, today has turned into the best day of my life by far.

My spent cock slips out of her, but the moment is far from over. I muster what little energy I have left and roll onto my side, with Amber still safely tucked into my arms. It takes a moment for my belly to stop jiggling into her. She wraps her arm across my side and pulls herself closer against me, squeezing and caressing all these bumps and folds of fat which no one should ever have been subjected to.

I'm shocked she isn't trying to get away from me now that my purpose has been served. If she was just horny, then surely, my work here is done? All I'm contributing to the situation now is the sweat I'm defiling her flawless body with. It's all so wrong, and yet she seems oblivious to it.

Amber looks at me lazily and caresses my hair, before leaning in and giving me a peck on the lips. Such a sweet gesture, loving, even though I did nothing to deserve it.

"This was your first time, wasn't it?"

I'm so shocked at her question, and unsure what to say. Though that does clear up my earlier doubts about whether we'd already done it at night and I just couldn't remember.

"Was it that obvious?" I ask at last.

She smiles and shakes her head. "No, you were amazing. It's just that I overheard the guys talking shit at the party."

I can't help but wonder what all she already knows about me, while I know very little about her.

"Where did you come from all of a sudden? Who are you?"

"Just someone who found the channel and developed a little crush. Couldn't get you out of my mind, so finally, I decided to seek you out. I couldn't let those assholes carry on as they were at your expense, anyway."

What sort of a person develops a crush on a guy whose only contribution to humanity has been a barrage of humiliating YouTube videos?

Our bodies are sticky, but I can't bear to let go of her. Once I do, she'll never let me hold her again, I'm certain of it.

"I've not seen you before last night, I think. Not at any other party. I would have remembered." Of course, I would have. She possesses the kind of beauty you simply can't forget.

She shakes her head. "I don't really like parties, most of the time."

"What do you like?" I ask.

"Music festivals, video games, comic book conventions."

Her answers blow my mind. "You cosplay?"

"Sure, with the right company." That sounds a lot like an invitation I'm going to have a hard time refusing. Whereas I've spent the past year or so casting off all those geeky pursuits in order to fit into the frat bro lifestyle, she seems completely unapologetic about her interests. How refreshing.

"Where have you been all my life?" I ask.

"Tucked away at home with my head in a book, mostly." She grins at me.

I let out a chuckle and marvel at how light my chest feels. I could look at her pretty face for the rest of my life if she'll let me. Will she? In fact, the longer I stare into her eyes, the more I feel my heart come to life. Are these the famous butterflies people talk about? Like the most intense nerves you've ever felt, only in a good way?

My phone rings somewhere in the distance, threatening to interrupt our moment of eye contact.

"I'm not going to pick up," I tell her.

"Good boy."

She smiles again, and my heart skips another few beats. I still don't get why she's here with me, but I'm trying my damndest not to question it any longer, so instead, I ask about her subjects. We chat some more, we laugh, but most of all, we carry on holding and caressing one another while staring into each other's eyes. As if it's the most normal thing in the world. It isn't, though. It's precious and rare and magical and completely undeserved.

I wish for this morning to never end. And once it does, I'd give anything to be able to do it all again. My life in exchange for an entire night with Amber.

"I think we're going to need another shower soon, huh?" she says, while running the tip of her index finger through my damp chest hair.

I know she's right, but the prospect of leaving this bed fills me with dread.

"What's wrong?" she asks, alerting me to the fact that I have zero game. Zero chance of playing it cool. Girls hate clingy, needy guys, don't they?

I shake my head, but finally, I can't stop myself from asking that one question that's been on my mind all along. "What's the upside for you?"

"This is the upside," she says, while resting her hand on my flabby chest and leaning in for yet another lazy kiss. Just like that, my cock twitches. *Jesus, again?*

She smiles against my mouth and nibbles on my bottom lip. My heart starts to race and my breaths speed up uncontrollably. I need a drink or five, just to calm myself down again.

"Tell me; do you eat like you drink?" she whispers.

I don't know why that question turns me on further. Oh yeah, it's because she's reaching downward and wrapping her fingers around my already partially firm shaft. It dulls the fresh ache in my crotch, but only slightly.

"Kind of," I say.

She smiles and licks her lips. "I want to make you a good, big breakfast. And then…"

Amazing, how she continues to take my breath away. "Why?" I wonder.

"I want to make you happy." The way she emphasizes the word 'happy' hints at something deeper; dirtier.

"Seeing you happy makes me happy," I respond. What a cliché, yet I absolutely mean it; subtext and all. Just the memory of the satisfied expression on her face when she lowered herself onto my cock earlier could make me cum all over again. I've never seen anything as enchanting.

"Making you something to eat would make me happy," she says. "Breakfast first, and then a shower. Together."

God, have mercy. She's fondling my balls now. It should be weird since nobody has ever touched me there before, but it's not. It blows my mind. I couldn't refuse her a damn thing right now.

"I don't want to let you go," I whisper, while placing my hand possessively on her hip.

She grinds her thigh against my crotch, taking my breath away.

"I'll make it worth your while. How many eggs?" she asks. "Come on it'll help take care of that hangover as well."

She's relentless! I wonder how to respond. Conservatively, so I don't come across as a complete pig?

Her eyes are wide with anticipation while I think of a response that won't disappoint her either way.

"Six?" she urges.

I keep quiet, wondering just what the hell I'm supposed to say. Will I invite judgement if I'm honest? Then again, she's seen me do what I do. Those videos are the whole reason she's here right now; in my bed.

"Eight?" She purses her lips. "Ten? Bacon? Sausages? I spotted some in the fridge."

Finally, I nod. "Sure, whatever you want."

She starts to stir, but I refuse to take my hand off her. She playfully pinches my side. "I can't cook in bed, can I?"

"No, but…"

"How about…" She wiggles her eyebrows and starts to peel the t-shirt off herself, prompting me to loosen my grip on her pretty quickly. Oh my God, she's so hot. I still can't believe she's here with me.

"You can watch me while I cook. Naked."

Hedonist

I still have nothing much to say, but obviously I can't refuse.

This morning has gone so much better than I could have hoped. I've got Frank exactly where I want him. Our first time was quick, but it managed to scratch the itch I've felt for him ever since I first started watching the channel; at least for the moment.

And now…

I'm naked in his kitchen, juggling three frying pans to prepare a breakfast of champions. He's watching me intently from the small round dining table, which is exactly what I wanted. The only thing I don't like about this situation is that he's too clothed for my liking. But I'm about to change that.

"Okay, breakfast is served," I say, while placing a hugely loaded plate of eggs, bacon and sausages in front of him.

He seemingly can't decide where to look. At the food I've prepared, which - admittedly - smells mouth-watering, or at my naked chest. I lean over and guide his face upwards to kiss him on the lips.

"Enjoy," I whisper.

"I will." I take a seat on the other chair and just observe him.

He pauses when he notices my eyes on him. "You're not having breakfast? There's plenty."

I smile and shake my head. "I'm not really that hungry… for food. I'd much rather watch you finish it all, only…"

"Only, what?"

"I'd like you to even the playing field." I gesture down at his big body, as yet hidden underneath the t-shirt and shorts. "Get naked for me?"

He licks his lips and puts his fork back down. While he slowly starts to pull his t-shirt over his head, I place my foot up on the chair next to me and spread.

My right hand travels downward. Sure enough, I'm still dripping wet. This lady boner isn't going to take care of itself.

I dip my finger into my pussy just once to coat it in our mixed juices, and start rubbing my clit in a circular motion.

Frank, meanwhile, has taken a seat again after discarding his cum stained shorts on the floor.

"Oh God," he mumbles, while observing me tease myself.

"Your food's going to get cold," I tell him.

He grabs his fork again and starts to eat. It's obvious his attention has been diverted, because he barely even chews before he swallows each hurried bite.

"You like it?" I ask.

"I love it, Amber. And the eggs too."

I love his sense of humour. That deserves a reward.

I bring my index and middle finger to my mouth and suck on them before plunging them deeply into my wet pussy.

He shifts awkwardly in his seat, then freezes with the fork halfway between the plate and his mouth. Obviously, he was already sporting a semi before I started cooking. Now, he's grown to his former impressive length and girth. Round two is going to be mind-blowing. For both of us.

"Eat up, baby," I remind him. "It's all for you."

His movements speed up. Forkful after forkful of eggs and sausages find their way into his mouth. He washes it down with large gulps of milk from the big pitcher I'd found earlier. Everything a growing boy needs. And he's definitely growing for me.

Now that he's fully on display for me, I can see the subtle changes in his physique as he carries on eating. The plate and humongous mug get emptier, and my decadent prince grows fuller and fatter.

I can see it in his eyes as well as his movements as they get lazier and slower. But most of all I can see it in his belly as it fills up and expands. He was mainly just squishy and wobbly before. Not that that's a bad thing; I love squishy.

But now, the skin around his abdomen has become tauter and he's even starting to show a few stretch marks at the sides. It's obvious where all this goodness is going. His body is going to have to work hard to digest it all, but that's okay. I'll be here to help. For as long as it takes.

"Starting to feel full?" I ask, while tapping my clit gently with the tip of my index finger and squirming in my seat as a result.

God, he turns me on. It would take absolutely nothing for me to finish myself off right now. But I'm intent on keeping my arousal teetering just near the edge of control for as long as I can.

"Yeah," he leans back and tries to catch his breath. His breathing has grown louder and more laboured; it's the only sound in the room right now, save for that creaky old chair he's torturing.

"I'm not buying it. After all the beer I've seen you put away last night." I smile.

"Doesn't it bother you? You're so fit, and I'm… this." He huffs and puffs as he shifts in his seat, no doubt trying to find a position that's more comfortable for his growing gut. I so want to feel it; to see how hard and full it's getting underneath all that luscious fat, but I resist the temptation for now and carry on teasing myself.

"Bother me? This is all part of the game, baby. That big appetite of yours gets me even wetter."

His eyes narrow a bit as his right hand drops the fork and rests on his huge, pudgy thigh, just inches away from his growing cock which by now is mostly obscured by his overgrown gut. I let out an involuntary moan as I watch him touch himself for the first time, but then I focus on the goal again.

"You're not going to finish?" I breathe.

"Oh, I'll finish."

"The food."

"Right," he says. But he doesn't stop pumping himself. His whole body shudders with every stroke. From his luxuriously padded arms to his saggy man tits, drum-like belly and even his flabby thighs. Everything shifts and moves along with his hand, driving me crazy with anticipation.

I shake my head. "Finish your food and I'll let you cum in me again."

His eyelids flag and he stifles a groan. "I'm so full I could just burst."

Somewhere in the distance, his phone rings again, but neither of us pay it any attention.

"I want you to. Into my pussy," I whisper.

He pauses for a moment and tries but fails to take a deep breath. He's going to need a hand; or at least some physical encouragement.

So, I get up and take a couple of steps in his direction, resting my hand appreciatively on his big belly. It's pretty solid and full, just as I thought. Lovely. His eyes widen while he waits for my next move.

"Very nice, Frank. You're doing so well. And there's not much left at all," I say, pointing at the plate, which is only a quarter of the way full now.

He's still silent; passive, except for his urgent, shallow breaths. So, this is what he's like up close after stuffing himself like a pig. The sound is already glorious, but I have a way of making even sweeter music.

I feed him a few forkfuls myself now, and watch him chew and swallow. Progress is slow. Little beads of sweat start to collect on his brow. All this eating for my pleasure, it must be such hard work, but I'm not going to back down.

"Don't you want to skip ahead to your reward?" I ask.

He grunts approvingly when I feed him another

mouthful and fondle his thick cock with my other hand. Oh, he loves it. He's shifting in his chair again, trying to get me to touch him harder, but I only tease him; I don't give him the firm hand job he desires.

After letting out a series of little belches, I hand him the fork back and get down on my knees in between his thighs.

Beautiful they are. Fluffy pale skin accentuates the multiple rolls of fat that his years of binge eating have formed on his inner thighs. I squeeze them along the way, before grabbing his dick firmly at last.

He cries out when I lean in and allow myself a first taste of the pre-cum already gracing the tip of his cock.

"Oh god, Amber," he gasps. It's obvious he's got his mouth full as well. He's finishing all the food for me, just as I demanded.

The only downside is that I can't see it from down here. My view of his face is obscured by all this luxurious flesh that's solely mine to play with. He leans back in the creaky chair, allowing me to take him into my mouth fully now, sucking on his rich cock and enjoying the resulting shudder in his hips and thighs.

Oh, he's amazing. The best and biggest I've ever had the privilege of playing with. I don't know why I didn't try to find him sooner. I should have realised that this was always going to be the inevitable end result of our meeting. I should have known he was always going to be mine.

The scraping of a fork against the plate signals that mealtime is almost over, although mine has just begun.

He reaches for the back of my head and grabs a fistful of hair. I love it. I've got him exactly as desperate as I want him to be. All I seek now is his complete satisfaction as well as mine.

"Stop, or I'll cum again," he groans.

While a part of me would love to swallow whatever he's got to offer, I do pause and pull away.

"Do you want to cum inside of me again?" I ask. "Or on my tits?"

He moans loudly; this time without me even touching him. He guides my face upwards, past these parts of his lower torso which he himself probably hasn't seen in quite a while.

"I want to make *you* cum first this time," he growls. "Tell me what to do."

Just like that, I'm nearly done for. So, he wasn't lying when he hinted that my enjoyment gives him pleasure too. He's very eager to please indeed.

I get up in front of him, slowly enough to lick and nibble my way all across his beautifully stuffed body until I reach his big, chubby face, cupping it with both hands. The way in which he's looking at me has changed from before. There's a certainty in his eyes now. He knows what we're about to do, because it's meant to be.

He's already emptied his balls into me once today and marked me as his. The change in him is undeniable. From now on, I'll belong to him for as long as he'll carry on wanting me.

He wraps his arms around me and positions me in between his thighs just like in the bedroom earlier, then he lets go, only to put his big, fleshy hand over my naked breast. With that simple gesture, he claims me as his own. It makes my heart skip a few beats.

"You're a dream come true, Amber."

I whimper when his other hand finds its way to the wetness between my folds and a fingertip brushes ever so softly against my entrance. I rock my hips into his hand, coaxing his finger into me.

He starts to move it in and out; slowly, tentatively. It feels glorious. I love how his finger is much thicker than my own.

"Fuck you're good at that," I moan.

His movements speed up just a little. He leans forward, huffing and grunting a bit as he does so, then takes one of my nipples into his mouth and sucks on it. It feels so good. So perfect. My heart is already racing. I feel like a million butterflies have invaded the inside of my tummy and are now fighting to break free.

I keep on moving my hips to speed up the rhythm of his finger, but he keeps on maintaining the same pace. He's still sucking on my tit, running his tongue across the nipple and making me squirm. His finger is slipping in and out of me at a steady pace; not enough to make me cum yet, but enough to drive me crazy with pleasure.

But eventually, he pulls away and leans back in his chair to catch his breath. He's too full to keep going like this. Bending over like that is obviously putting too much pressure on his insides, which are still struggling to contain that big breakfast I'd made for him.

My turn to lean across him, rubbing his strained belly

with the palm of my hand. His eyes close partially.

"You're so big and fat; I love it," I whisper.

I reach further down and find his fat cock already waiting for me. Still standing proud. Still close to bursting, just like the rest of him.

"No," he huffs. "You first this time."

I smile and lean on his gut just enough to add even more pressure. "But you're so full; so helpless! How will you stop me from finishing you off right now?"

He growls disapprovingly and pushes me away a little. Then, he takes a deep breath and heaves himself up from the chair while stifling a groan. He grabs my ass and pulls me into him, then seeks out my lips with his. Hungry and eager; he kisses me, licks me, tastes me fully. I have to stand on my tiptoes just to reach him properly now that he's upright.

This new assertiveness he's developed just now turns my insides to jelly. He might have started off shy, but that's obviously a thing of the past now.

He squeezes my ass cheeks, then lifts me up just enough for my feet to raise off the ground by a foot or so. All the while, we're still making out. I love how small he makes me feel. He's got me up in the air, and it seemingly makes no difference to him.

I guess compared to him, my weight is pretty insignificant anyway. I'm what; one-twenty? I wonder how long it took him to gain the last hundred and twenty pounds on his generous frame? A couple of years? I would have liked to see the progression of how all this weight ended up on him. And what all he had to eat to make it happen.

But still, it's the right here and now that counts. He's so big. So perfect. And pretty damn strong, to be able to move all that bulk around every day. He can do what he likes with me; that's for sure.

Now I'm the one who's helpless, though entirely willing for whatever is yet to come.

He sets me down on the table. The empty plate and cutlery end up on the floor, shattering against the tiles. Neither of us pay it any mind.

This time *he* pushes *me* down onto my back, spreads my thighs and dips two fingers into me. I squirm up into his hand, trying to get him to fill me up more. But as thick as his fingers are, they're no match compared to what I really want: his dick.

"Who are you calling helpless, huh?" he growls, while he fingers me deeply with his right hand, and squeezes my breast with his other. "

It's all too much for me. I can hardly keep my eyes open any longer. My breaths have sped up out of control, matching the relentless racing of my heart.

"I am, Frank. I'm helpless. Whatever you want to do to me, I'm yours!" I moan.

He positions himself between my thighs and rubs the tip of his dick against my slick cunt. Pleasure jolts through me, threatening to overwhelm me even further. So close to salvation, and yet it's still so out of reach!

"I want you, baby. Don't torture me," I plead.

He inches forward, lifting his big, taut belly up a bit so our bodies have room to merge. Then, he starts to push into me, slowly at first.

My pussy eagerly accepts his rock-solid offering, and I can't keep quiet anymore.

"Oh, Frank! I love it, keep going!"

He does; beautifully so.

He hooks his arms under my knees, anchoring me in place on the table, and starts to thrust. With his belly on top of me, resting on my lower abdomen, I am thoroughly pinned in place. It's so heavy. So full. His body is everything I hoped it would be. Everything I fantasised about while watching him online.

He's setting the pace he likes; harder, faster. My mind grows clouded; so overcome am I with pleasure.

This is what I'd been hoping for. This is what I dreamed about every night. Even last night at the party, when I first saw him, visions like this moment right now entered my mind, driving me crazy with lust.

He's perfection personified. Slamming into me, his big, bulky body crushing against me with every stroke. I rest my hands on his belly, rubbing, squishing, fondling him to my heart's content.

It was nice being on top of him. And I intend to do that again sometime when we're both in a state to last longer. But this right here pushes me to a whole other level of pleasure.

I have the best view. Of Frank's adorable chubby face, sweating, reddening with exertion as he struggles to move his stuffed body in new and exciting ways, just to please me.

And please me, he does.

Every time he goes in deep, I can't stop myself from moaning and whimpering his name. From digging my fingernails into the gorgeously pillowy skin of his love handles, which seem to go on forever. I'm probably scratching him up quite badly, but he doesn't seem to care.

He's fully locked onto me. Staring at me with complete focus. Fighting to go on, when his body wants nothing more than to rest and digest.

I can understand. It must be difficult. But he's trying so hard just for me. It brings tears to my eyes.

"Baby, you're perfect," he grunts.

"You are," I respond.

I reach for his face; it's quite a stretch, but I manage it somehow. He's wet and sticky with sweat, but that hardly bothers me. I run my thumb over his lower lip. God, his lips are so kissable. Too bad they're out of my reach.

He keeps going, giving me the fuck of a lifetime right here on top of his kitchen table. I'm conflicted. Desperate for my release, yet unwilling to let the moment end too quickly.

But soon, as his right hand finds my boob again, and starts thumbing my nipple, I hardly have a choice anymore. It tickles deliciously, sending me spiralling out of control.

"Oh God, I'm going to-" I cry.

He moves with renewed vigour. Grinding into me as deeply as possible with every thrust. It's enough to drive me wild for him.

"Frank, cum with me!" I scream. "I can't stop!"

He closes his eyes, and his formerly tense expression starts to relax. He's so gorgeous. My dream. My man.

I surrender to my orgasm. It fills every one of my veins with a heat I've never known before. So comforting; so satisfying. I couldn't have done it better myself. Not with my hands, nor with my favourite toy. My eyes close involuntarily, but as I lose my vision, I gain a whole new sense of understanding of everything that's going on in our bodies. Of every beat of my heart. Every breath we take. Every shiver and tremble in our near-spent muscles.

All goes still around us. He's stopped moving now too, except for that insistent throbbing deep inside my cunt. It can only mean one thing. This is the sensation of his cock unloading into me, for the second time today. Without a condom, he marks me as his yet again.

I muster what little energy I have left to reach for him. To massage his belly, which has got to be aching after all this exercise so soon after a huge meal.

He whimpers softly, and releases the previously iron grip on my legs. I look up at him, admiring his handsome face. He is my hero; now and forever. If only he'll carry on wanting me.

His bottom lip is shaking now. Sweat dripping down his hairline, and running along the side of his face in streaks. He's obviously exhausted, and hanging on by sheer willpower.

I noticed the same even last night. When he was so wasted, most guys would have just given up and allowed sleep to take over, he did his best to stumble home with me. He even made it through the shower I insisted on without any complaints.

Frank isn't like other guys, obviously. He's the best. He's mine.

And now that he's taken care of me, I owe it to him to return the favour.

I raise myself onto my elbows.

"Baby, I know I said we'd need another shower, but why don't we just get back into bed instead?" I whisper.

His eyes open, and he blinks a few times. "I keep expecting to wake up from this dream," he mumbles.

I grin at him. "You're so cute."

He takes a step back, allowing me to get up as well. The first thing I do once I've got my feet back on the ground is wrap my arms around him. They don't go all the way, but I wouldn't want them to.

"You're like a big teddy bear, you know that?" I ask.

He's still trying to catch his breath and failing. "If you say so."

Once I let go of him, I take his hand and lead him back into the bedroom, where I gesture at him to get back under the covers. The effect is almost instant; his eyes flag once he hits the mattress. And my heart overflows.

"What about you?" he asks.

I cock my head to the side and look at him for a moment. What an inviting sight. Such a big man in such a comparatively small bed. I don't know how it's still in one piece underneath his impressive weight. It's quite comical, actually, and makes me smile.

"Scoot over," I say.

He does; turning onto his side with just enough room to spare for me to fit in ahead of him. I get under the duvet and let out a contented sigh.

"I don't know why you want this; any of it," he says.

I don't respond, I just turn around and bury my face in his chest hair. It tickles and makes me smile even more. Then I pull back and look up at him again. I can't get enough of just looking at him. At his beautiful body. Into his beautiful eyes.

"Does it matter why anyone wants what they want?" I ask.

He shrugs. "I suppose not."

"I just know I want to be here. With you," I continue.

"Promise this isn't just a dream?"

"Of course it's a dream. Just not one either of us will wake up from," I say.

"I hope not. I never knew-" he doesn't finish his sentence, just stares into my eyes.

The way he's looking at me melts my heart yet again.

"You're not just going to disappear on me once I fall asleep, are you?" he asks.

I shake my head. "I'll be here. Right next to you."

He caresses my hair and holds me like before. After the first time we did it in this bed.

"Good. I wouldn't know what I'd do otherwise." He blinks lazily. It's obvious he's hit his limits.

Who knew? Litres of beer didn't seem to affect him

much, but a big breakfast followed by a good fuck? My baby is done for.

I start massaging his stuffed belly, gently at first. It's so hard, he must be feeling so uncomfortable. His eyes shut and he sinks deeper into his pillow.

"So good," he whispers.

"Sleep now," I say, while rubbing his distended stomach in firmer, circular movements, working my way all around as far as I can reach. Even though it's not strictly sexual, it still satisfies me in ways even that mind-blowing orgasm couldn't have done.

His breaths slow. His expression relaxes. But I don't stop, not for a while.

I keep massaging him, whispering sweet nothings at him, and watching over him. How strange life can be… One night you're heading to a party, which totally isn't your usual scene, hoping beyond hope to hook up with a guy you don't know; whom you've never even met before. And the next morning you're in his bed, wondering how you ever managed without him.

The longer I carry on looking at him, the more certain I am that things worked out exactly how they were supposed to.

"Sweet dreams," I whisper. "Regain your strength. Because come lunchtime, we're going to do it all over again."

Although he's obviously asleep, he moans softly at

my words. His hips twitch in my direction just enough

for me to notice. I've created a monster. Good, because I am one too.

75

ABOUT THE AUTHOR

Dear Reader,

If you came across me in real life, you'd never guess the kind of filth I like to read and write. Cleverly disguised as a boring office worker, the drudgery of my 9-to-5 only because bearable because of my vivid and explicit imagination. I like fat guys and I cannot lie. In my world, bigger (fatter) is always better. It's been that way for as long as I can remember.

Thanks for reading this story, one of hopefully many of my published sexual fantasies. My stories revolve around one common theme: really big men and the women who can't help but lust for them.

Although I like porn just fine, it's nearly impossible to find it in the flavour that I desire. The written word allows me to explore a world of lush excess that mainstream adult entertainment just cannot provide. When I started writing, I soon discovered the beauty of having a catalog of erotica out there to satisfy my own lustful needs. This is a passion project more than a money-grab.

So, first and foremost, my writing is for me. But perhaps there are other women (or even men) out there who share my tastes; my fetishes and fantasies? My fascination with the larger male form, and sexualisation of food (especially overeating). If that sounds like something you'll wank off to, you've come to the right place.

xxx Hedonist

To find out more, check:

- ❖ eXplicitTales.com

www.ingramcontent.com/pod-product-compliance
Lightning Source LLC
Chambersburg PA
CBHW070511170726
48291CB00008B/2707